This
PJ BOOK
belongs to

_____

_____

PJ Library®

JEWISH BEDTIME STORIES and SONGS

SAMMY SPIDER'S
FIRST **PASSOVER**

SYLVIA A. ROUSS

illustrated by

KATHERINE JANUS KAHN

KAR-BEN
PUBLISHING

To my husband Jeff
for his inspiration, support, and encouragement.
—S.A.R.

To David
—K.J.K.

Text copyright © 1995 by Sylvia A. Rouss
Illustrations copyright © 1995 by Katherine Janus Kahn

KAR-BEN PUBLISHING
A division of Lerner Publishing Group, Inc.
241 First Avenue North
Minneapolis, MN 55401 USA
800-4KARBEN

For reading levels and more information,
look up this title at www.karben.com.

Library of Congress Cataloging-in-Publication Data

Rouss, Sylvia A.
   Sammy Spider's first Passover / Sylvia Rouss : illustrated by
Katherine Janus Kahn.
      p.   cm.
   Summary: A young spider makes a special contribution to a
family's Passover seder.
   ISBN 978-0-929371-81-8 (lib. bdg. : alk. paper)
   ISBN 978-0-929371-82-5 (pbk. : alk. paper)
   ISBN 978-0-7613-8934-7 (eBook)
   [1. Passoverl—Fiction. 2. Seder—Fiction. 3. Spiders—
Fiction.] I. Kahn, Katherine, ill. II. Title.
PZ7.R7622San 1995
[E]—dc20   94-41880

Manufactured in Hong Kong
1 – PN – 11/1/14

031525.4K/B594

A Book of
SHAPES

Sammy Spider was fast asleep in his web high up on the Shapiros' living room ceiling. As the warm spring sun shone through an open window, Sammy snuggled deeper into his cozy web.

A sudden
swishing noise
startled him
awake.

"Mother!" he screamed.

"A monster has broken our web!"

Sammy scurried across
the ceiling and hid
in a corner.

Mrs. Spider hurried to
comfort him. "Don't
worry, Sammy. That
'monster' is called a
broom, and Mr. Shapiro
is using it to dust
the ceiling."

"Each spring the Shapiros give their house a special cleaning to prepare for Passover. Springtime is a perfect time for us to make a new web."

"I don't know how to make a web," Sammy said sadly.

"I'm going to teach you," said his mother, giving him a big hug.

"Will we celebrate Passover, too?" asked Sammy.

"Silly little Sammy," laughed Mrs. Spider. "Spiders don't celebrate Passover. Spiders spin webs."

"We begin by spinning one thread."

"Then we spin a second and a third. Finally we spin a fourth to make a square."

But Sammy wasn't listening. "What is Mr. Shapiro putting on the table?" he asked.

"That's called matzah," Mrs. Spider replied. "Tonight is the first night of Passover, and the Shapiros will have a special meal called a seder."

Then Mrs. Shapiro brought in a big platter with a roasted egg and bone, parsley, charoset, and bitter herbs.

"That's called a seder plate," Mrs. Spider explained. "The Shapiros will eat special foods at their seder."

"Do spiders eat special foods for Passover?" asked Sammy.

"Silly little Sammy," answered his mother. "Spiders don't celebrate Passover."

"Spiders eat flies and other insects. To catch them we spin a web, and I need your help. Watch me attach a circle to the inside of our web."

But Sammy wasn't listening. He was hovering on a silky strand above the table, watching the Shapiros at their seder. CRUNCH, went the matzah, as Mr. Shapiro broke it in half. Sammy watched him wrap one of the broken pieces in a bright, red napkin.

When Josh wasn't looking, Mr. Shapiro hid it on top of the bookcase.

Sammy climbed back up to the ceiling. "Mother," he asked, "why did Mr. Shapiro hide the matzah?"

"It's called the afikomen," Mrs. Spider answered. "After the meal, Josh will try to   find it. If he does, he'll get a prize."

"What fun," Sammy said. "Can I play, too?"

"Silly little Sammy," said his mother. "Spiders don't celebrate Passover. Spiders spin webs. And I really need your help to spin a triangle inside the circle."

But Sammy wasn't listening. He looked longingly at the hidden afikomen. "All right," sighed Mrs. Spider. "You may watch the seder for awhile."

Sammy quickly crossed the ceiling and stopped right above the bookshelf, as Josh finished reciting the Four Questions. He listened as the family sang Passover songs and took turns reading the story of Moses, who led the Jews to freedom.

The Shapiros began their seder meal.

Sammy had never seen so much food!

At last it was time to search for the afikomen. Sammy wished he could help, but he remembered his mother's words. "Spiders don't celebrate Passover."

Swinging from a strand of webbing, he watched as Josh searched every corner of the room.

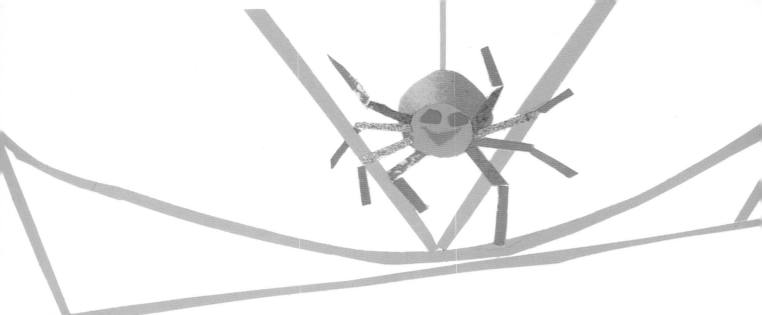

When Josh neared the bookshelf, Sammy got excited.

Something shiny caught Josh's eye. It was an amazing little web, with a beautiful Jewish star inside.

"Wow!" breathed Josh. As he went closer to look, he spotted the afikomen, just below the glistening web.

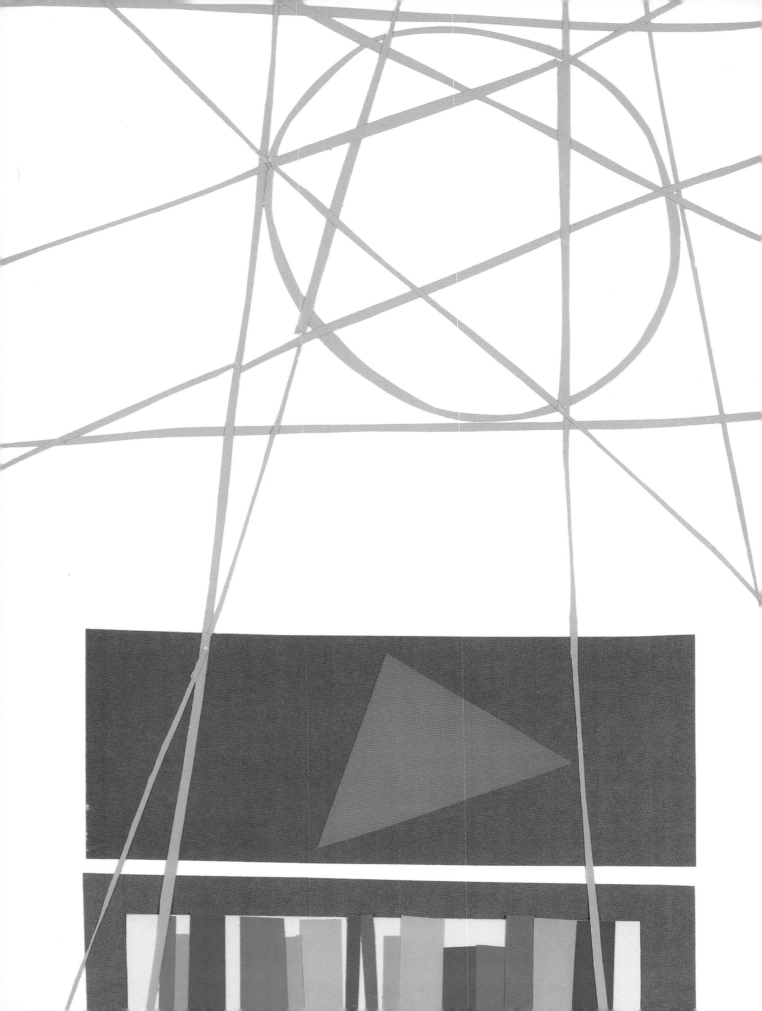

WOW

"I
FOUND
IT!"

he squealed.

Sammy glowed with pride. "I did it, Mother! I helped Josh find the afikomen."

"And you also spun a beautiful web," Mrs. Spider answered. "You used all the shapes I taught you."

In his excitement, Sammy didn't even know that he had spun a web. As he looked back at the bookshelf, he beamed. "It was easy, Mother! You make a square, a circle, and a triangle.

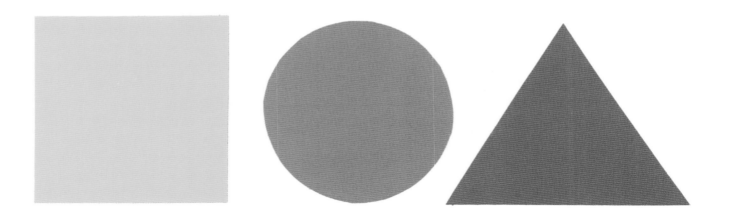

Then you PASS OVER with another triangle. That's how spiders celebrate Passover!"

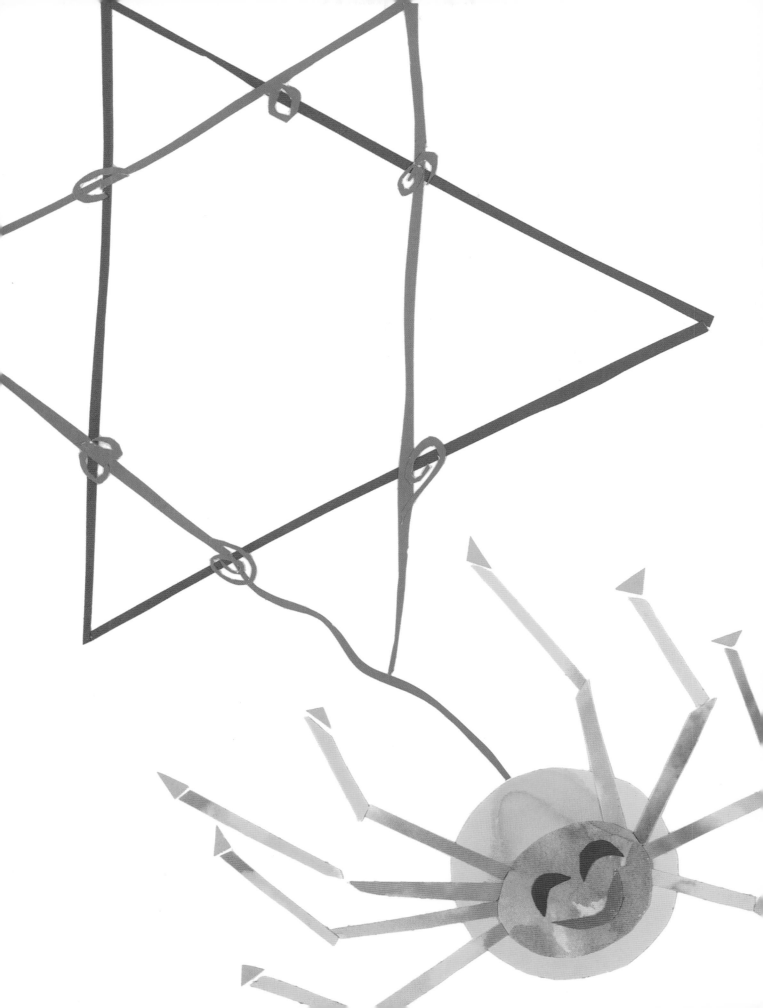